12/95

Other books by
PATRICIA COOMBS

Dorrie and the Amazing Magic Elixir
Dorrie and the Birthday Eggs
Dorrie and the Blue Witch
Dorrie and the Fortune Teller
Dorrie and the Goblin
Dorrie and the Halloween Plot
Dorrie and the Haunted House
Dorrie and the Weather-Box
Dorrie and the Witch Doctor
Dorrie and the Witch's Imp
Dorrie and the Wizard's Spell
Lisa and the Grompet
Molly Mullett
Mouse Café

Patricia Coombs
The Magic Pot

Lothrop, Lee & Shepard Company

A Division of William Morrow & Company, Inc. New York

Library of Congress Cataloging in Publication Data

Coombs, Patricia.

The Magic Pot.

SUMMARY: A demon in the guise of a magic pot outwits a greedy, rich man and brings wealth and happiness to a poor old fellow and his wife.

[1. Fairy tales] I. Title.

PZ8.C7883Mag   [E]   76-54876

ISBN 0-688-41792-2

ISBN 0-688-51792-7 lib. bdg.

To Edna

Once there was a funny little demon. He looked around and he looked around. "Hucka-pucka, hucka-pucka," said the demon, and turned himself into a black iron pot. He sat himself down at the side of the road. The road went by a little hut where an old man and his old wife lived.

In a little while, along came the poor old man. He had been to the rich man's house to beg for work and a bit of bread. He saw the pot. "Well, something is better than nothing," he said, and he took it home.

His old wife met him at the door. "Did you get some work and a bit of bread?"

"I did not," said the old man. "All I got was hard words and a few hard whacks. 'If you're too old to work, then you're too old to eat,' they said."

"What will become of us?" cried the old woman. "We have sold the pig. We have sold the cow. We have only ourselves and the cat left." And she began to cry.

"Don't cry," said the old man. "Look, I found this pot beside the road. In a little while, I will go and sell it." And the old man lay down to rest.

The old wife put the pot on the shelf, took the broom and began to sweep. The pot turned around on its three iron legs. It hopped off the shelf.

"Hucka-pucka," said the pot.

"Where will you hucka-pucka to?" cried the old woman.

"To the rich man's house and back again," said the pot. And hucka-pucka, hucka-pucka, out the door and down the road went the pot.

Hucka-pucka, into the rich man's kitchen it went.

"Ah ha!" said the cook. "Just the pot I need to hold all this good stew!" Into the pot went the stew.

"Hucka-pucka," said the pot.

"Where will you hucka-pucka to?" cried the cook.

"To a place the rich have never been," said the pot. And before the cook could grab it, the pot went back down the road toward the poor man's hut.

The poor old man was awake. His old wife was crying, for the pot was gone.

When they saw it come back, and smelled the good stew, they laughed for joy. They filled their bowls and ate until they could eat no more. They thanked the pot. The old woman washed it and the old man set it back on the shelf.

In a little while, the pot turned around on its three iron legs. It hopped off the shelf.

"Hucka-pucka," said the pot.

"Where will you hucka-pucka to?" said the old man.

"To the rich man's house and back again," said the pot. Out the door and down the road it went.

The door to the rich man's dairy was open. The dairymaid was churning butter. There was so much butter she had run out of tubs. Hucka-pucka, hucka-pucka, in came the pot.

"Ah ha!" cried the dairymaid. "Just the pot I need to put the butter in!" And she filled the pot with good, sweet butter.

"Hucka-pucka," said the pot.

"Where will you hucka-pucka to?" said the dairymaid.

"To a place the rich have never been," said the pot. Before the dairymaid could grab it, the pot went hucka-pucka, back down the road to the poor man's hut.

The old woman looked into the pot. Her eyes popped open. "Butter! Good, sweet butter! Some to eat and some to sell!" And she and the old man clapped for joy.

Off went the old man to trade some butter for eggs and bread. The old woman washed the pot. She hugged it and thanked it and put it on the shelf.

She sat down with her mending by the fire. The pot sat quietly for a little while. Then it turned on its legs and hopped off the shelf.

"Hucka-pucka," said the pot.

"Where will you hucka-pucka to?" said the old woman.

"To the rich man's house and back again," said the pot. Out the door and down the road to the rich man's house it went.

The pantry door was open. The butler was polishing the silver. Hucka-pucka, hucka-pucka, into the pantry went the pot. It stood very still.

"Ah ha!" cried the butler. "Just the pot I need to hold some of this silver!" And into the pot went silver spoons and knives and forks and cups and plates and bowls.

When it was full to the top, the pot said, "Hucka-pucka."

"Where will you hucka-pucka to?" said the butler.

"To a place the rich have never been," said the pot. Before the butler could stop it, down the road and back to the poor man's hut went the pot.

Hucka-pucka, hucka-pucka, in came the pot. When the old man and his wife saw the pot full of silver, they skipped for joy.

They took out the silver. They hugged the pot, and thanked it, and put it back on the shelf.

The old man took some of the silver and went off to trade it for a cow. The old woman put the rest of the silver away.

The pot rested for a little while. Then off the shelf it hopped.

"Hucka-pucka," said the pot.

"Where will you hucka-pucka to?" said the old woman.

"To the rich man's house and back again," said the pot. Out the door and down the road it went, hucka-pucka, hucka-pucka.

A window was open. Inside, the rich man was counting his gold and locking it up. Up hopped the pot and sat on the table.

"Ah ha!" cried the rich man. "Just the pot I need to hold the rest of this gold!" And into the pot he poured the gold.

"Hucka-pucka," said the pot.

"Where will you hucka-pucka to?" cried the rich man.

"To a place the rich have never been," said the pot. Off the table it hopped, and out the window. Hucka-pucka, hucka-pucka, down the road it went.

The rich man went running after it.

"Stop!" he yelled. "Come back with my gold!" But the rich man was too fat to run very far. He had to sit down to catch his breath.

Hucka-pucka, hucka-pucka, back to the hut went the pot.

The old man had traded some of the silver for a nice brown cow. He was bringing in a pail of milk when the pot danced through the door.

The old man and his old wife looked into the pot. They were so happy they danced for joy around and around the hut. The pot danced around with them. And so did the cat.

The old man and his old wife took the gold and put it away. They hugged the pot, and thanked it, and put it back on the shelf.

The pot sat for a little while, thinking. Then it turned around on its three iron legs and hopped off the shelf.

"Hucka-pucka," said the pot.

"There is no need," said the old man and his old wife. "You have brought us enough to last the rest of our days."

"All the same, hucka-pucka I must," said the pot.

"Where will you hucka-pucka to?" said the old man and his old wife.

"To the rich man's house, and I won't be back again," said the pot. And hucka-pucka, off he went.

The rich man was fishing in his pond. He saw the pot and he said, "Ah ha! Just the pot I need!"

But it wasn't fish he put into the pot. He began filling it with stones and mud from the pond. "You won't fool me again," yelled the rich man. And he dumped more and more mud and stones into the pot.

The pot began to hop up and down on its three iron legs. Then it began to swell up— bigger and bigger and bigger. As the rich man angrily stuffed more mud into it, the pot lifted him high into the air. Head over heels went the rich man, down into the pot full of mud. Into the mud went his fine clothes, his gold rings and chains.

"Help! Help!" cried the rich man, trying to get out. But it did him no good.

"Hucka-pucka," said the pot.

"Where will you hucka-pucka to?" spluttered the rich man, his mouth full of mud.

The pot just grinned, and hucka-pucka, hucka-pucka, off they went and were never seen again.

Patricia Coombs was born in Los Angeles, California and received her B.A. and M.A. from the University of Washington. She has illustrated all of her own books as well as those by other authors. Ms. Coombs lives with her husband, two daughters and a house full of pets in Waterford, Connecticut, where she enjoys gardening, sailing, and animal and bird life.